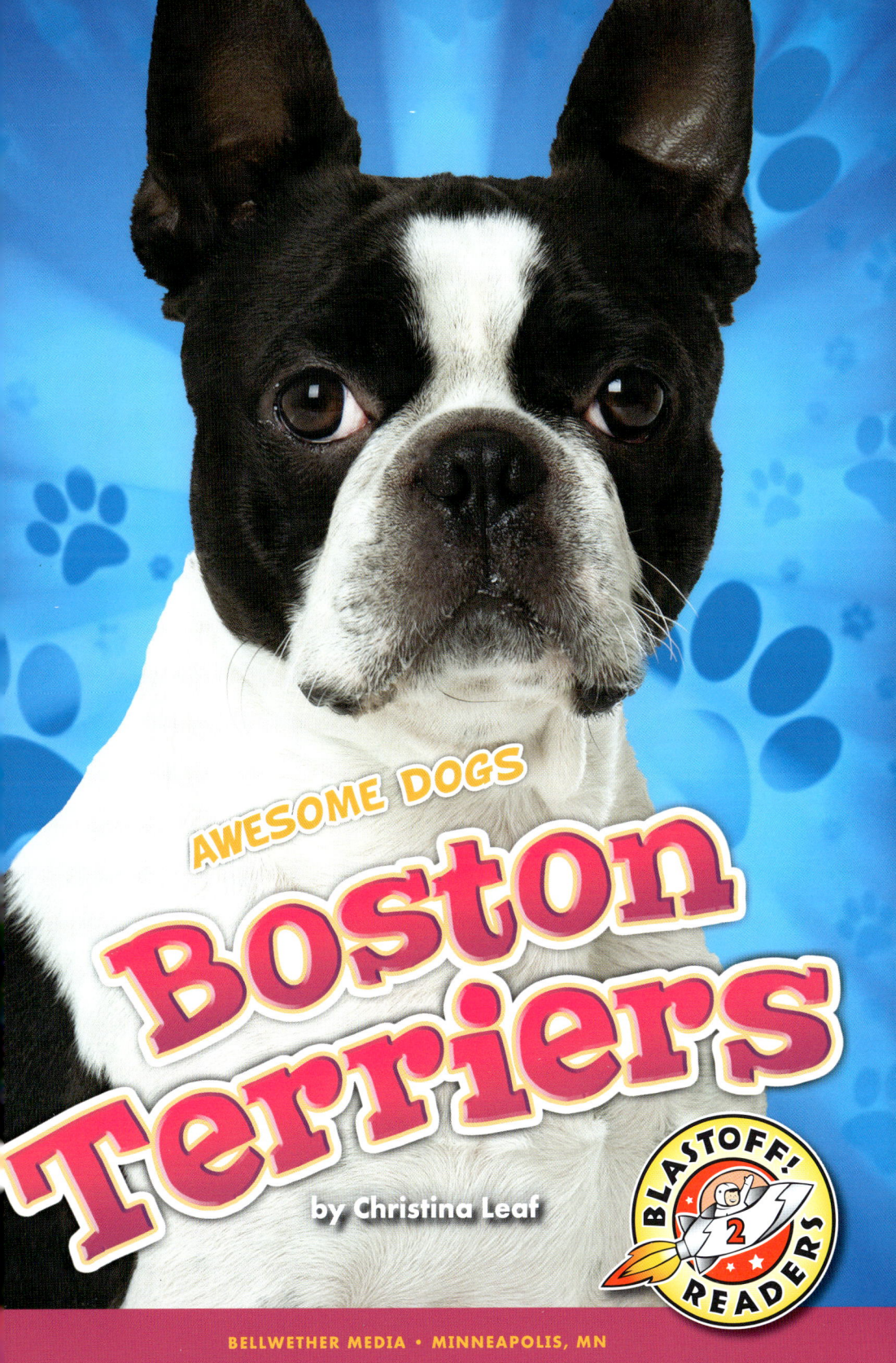

AWESOME DOGS

Boston Terriers

by Christina Leaf

BLASTOFF! READERS 2

BELLWETHER MEDIA • MINNEAPOLIS, MN

Note to Librarians, Teachers, and Parents:

Blastoff! Readers are carefully developed by literacy experts and combine standards-based content with developmentally appropriate text.

Level 1 provides the most support through repetition of high-frequency words, light text, predictable sentence patterns, and strong visual support.

Level 2 offers early readers a bit more challenge through varied simple sentences, increased text load, and less repetition of high-frequency words.

Level 3 advances early-fluent readers toward fluency through increased text and concept load, less reliance on visuals, longer sentences, and more literary language.

Level 4 builds reading stamina by providing more text per page, increased use of punctuation, greater variation in sentence patterns, and increasingly challenging vocabulary.

Level 5 encourages children to move from "learning to read" to "reading to learn" by providing even more text, varied writing styles, and less familiar topics.

Whichever book is right for your reader, Blastoff! Readers are the perfect books to build confidence and encourage a love of reading that will last a lifetime!

This edition first published in 2017 by Bellwether Media, Inc.

No part of this publication may be reproduced in whole or in part without written permission of the publisher. For information regarding permission, write to Bellwether Media, Inc., Attention: Permissions Department, 5357 Penn Avenue South, Minneapolis, MN 55419.

Library of Congress Cataloging-in-Publication Data

Names: Leaf, Christina, author.
Title: Boston Terriers / by Christina Leaf.
Description: Minneapolis, MN : Bellwether Media, Inc., 2017. | Series: Blastoff! Readers. Awesome Dogs | Includes bibliographical references and index. | Audience: Ages 5 to 8. | Audience: Grades K to 3.
Identifiers: LCCN 2016033338 (print) | LCCN 2016042915 (ebook) | ISBN 9781626175570 (hardcover : alk. paper) | ISBN 9781681032788 (ebook)
Subjects: LCSH: Boston terrier–Juvenile literature.
Classification: LCC SF429.B7 L43 2017 (print) | LCC SF429.B7 (ebook) | DDC 636.72–dc23
LC record available at https://lccn.loc.gov/2016033338

Text copyright © 2017 by Bellwether Media, Inc. BLASTOFF! READERS and associated logos are trademarks and/or registered trademarks of Bellwether Media, Inc. SCHOLASTIC, CHILDREN'S PRESS, and associated logos are trademarks and/or registered trademarks of Scholastic Inc.

Editor: Betsy Rathburn   Designer: Lois Stanfield

Printed in the United States of America, North Mankato, MN.

Table of Contents

What Are Boston Terriers?	4
History of Boston Terriers	12
Playful Pups	18
Glossary	22
To Learn More	23
Index	24

What Are Boston Terriers?

Boston terriers are charming dogs with fancy outfits. Their markings look like a **tuxedo**!

This led people to call the **breed** "the American Gentleman." They are also called Bostons.

Boston terrier **coats** are smooth and short. Most are black.

Less common colors are **seal** and **brindle**. Bostons have a white chest, **blaze**, and **muzzle**.

Boston terriers are small but **sturdy**. They weigh up to 25 pounds (11 kilograms).

Their tails are naturally short.

Boston terrier heads are square with short muzzles. The ears stick straight up.

Round, dark eyes make these dogs look friendly.

History of Boston Terriers

Boston terriers were first born in Boston, Massachusetts. They were one of the first United States breeds.

A dog named Judge started the breed. He came from a bulldog and an English white terrier.

Robert C. Hooper **bred** Judge around 1870. The puppy was popular!

Soon, more puppies strengthened the breed. Later, these new dogs were named Boston terriers.

In 1893, the **American Kennel Club** first included Boston terriers.

They are part of the **Non-Sporting Group**.

Playful Pups

Boston terriers love to play! But keep playtime short.

The dogs easily get too hot. Their short noses make breathing hard.

Friendly Bostons get along with everyone. They play with children and other pets.

Bostons are also cuddly. These gentle dogs love to be with people!

Glossary

American Kennel Club—an organization that keeps track of dog breeds in the United States

blaze—a stripe down the center of an animal's face; blazes are usually white.

bred—purposely mated two dogs to make puppies with certain qualities

breed—a type of dog

brindle—a solid coat color mixed with streaks or spots of another color

coats—the hair or fur covering some animals

muzzle—the nose and mouth of an animal

Non-Sporting Group—a group of dog breeds that do not usually hunt or work

seal—a color that appears black but looks reddish in sunlight

sturdy—strongly built

tuxedo—a fancy suit with a white shirt and black jacket

To Learn More

AT THE LIBRARY
Landau, Elaine. *Boston Terriers Are the Best!* Minneapolis, Minn.: Lerner, 2011.

Morey, Allan. *Boston Terriers.* North Mankato, Minn.: Capstone Press, 2017.

Wheeler, Jill C. *Boston Terriers.* Edina, Minn.: ABDO Pub., 2010.

ON THE WEB
Learning more about Boston terriers is as easy as 1, 2, 3.

1. Go to www.factsurfer.com.

2. Enter "Boston terriers" into the search box.

3. Click the "Surf" button and you will see a list of related web sites.

With factsurfer.com, finding more information is just a click away.

Index

American Kennel Club, 16
Boston, Massachusetts, 12
breathing, 19
bred, 14
breed, 5, 12, 13, 15
bulldog, 13
chest, 7
children, 20
coats, 6, 7
colors, 6, 7
ears, 10
English white terrier, 13
eyes, 11
heads, 9, 10
Hooper, Robert C., 14
Judge, 13, 14
life span, 9
markings, 4, 7, 9
muzzle, 7, 9, 10
name, 15

nicknames, 5
Non-Sporting Group, 17
noses, 19
pets, 20
play, 18, 20
puppy, 14, 15
size, 8, 9
tails, 9
trainability, 9
United States, 12

The images in this book are reproduced through the courtesy of: Dora Zett, front cover, pp. 6-7, 9; Jean Michel Labat/ ardea.com/ Pantheon/ SuperStock, pp. 4, 7 (right), 14, 16; Barbara von Hoffmann/ Alamy Stock Photo, pp. 4-5; TheresaSc, p. 7 (left); Julie Poole/ Animal Photography, p. 7 (center); Tierfotoagentur/ Alamy Stock Photo, pp. 8-9, 10, 11, 13, 18, 20; Roman Zhuravlev, pp. 14-15; blueumbrellastudios, p. 17; Dylan/ Stockimo/ Alamy Stock Photo, pp. 18-19; Cultura RM/ Alamy Stock Photo, p. 21.